SHARK BAIT!

Jeff Szpirglas
Danielle Saint-Onge

ILLUSTRATED BY
Dave Whamond

orca Echoes

ORCA BOOK PUBLISHERS

Text copyright © Jeff Szpirglas and Danielle Saint-Onge 2021
Illustrations copyright © Dave Whamond 2021

Published in Canada and the United States in 2021 by Orca Book Publishers.
orcabook.com

Library and Archives Canada Cataloguing in Publication
Shark bait! / Jeff Szpirglas, Danielle Saint-Onge ; illustrated by Dave Whamond.
Names: Szpirglas, Jeff, author. | Saint-Onge, Danielle, 1982– author. |
Whamond, Dave, illustrator.
Series: Orca echoes.
Description: Series statement: Orca echoes
Identifiers: Canadiana (print) 20200181068 | Canadiana (ebook) 20200181114 |
ISBN 9781459823679 (softcover) | ISBN 9781459823686 (PDF) |
ISBN 9781459823693 (EPUB)
Classification: LCC PS8637.Z65 S53 2021 | DDC jC813/.6—dc23

Library of Congress Control Number: 2020931813

Summary: In this partially illustrated early chapter book, a young girl who is
fascinated by sharks gets a chance to see one in real life while taking sailing lessons.

Orca Book Publishers is committed to reducing the consumption
of nonrenewable resources in the making of our books. We make
every effort to use materials that support a sustainable future.

Orca Book Publishers gratefully acknowledges the support for its publishing
programs provided by the following agencies: the Government of Canada,
the Canada Council for the Arts and the Province of British Columbia
through the BC Arts Council and the Book Publishing Tax Credit.

Cover artwork and interior illustrations by Dave Whamond
Author photo by Tim Basile

Printed and bound in Canada.

24 23 22 21 • 2 3 4 5

for Ruby and Léo

Chapter One

"Ugh. Why does it smell like a tuna sandwich gone bad?"

Orly looked up from her suitcase and saw her mother holding her nose. She was fanning the air with her hand. She looked like she might throw up.

Orly's mom looked around the room. "Did you leave your wet swimsuit under your bed again?"

Orly shook her head. "Nope!"

"Have you left last week's lunch in your room somewhere? It's happened before..."

Orly shook her head again. This time she had a smile on her face. "Nope!"

"Then what is that horrible smell?" asked her mother.

"Chum!"

"*Gum*? Gum doesn't smell that bad."

"No, Mom. Chum!" Orly lifted up a large clear plastic bag from her suitcase. The bag was full of fish heads, fins and guts.

Orly's mother looked again like she was going to be sick. "Why are you packing *that* in your luggage?"

"I told you, it's chum. We're going to need it."

"For what? You can't eat that on the drive."

"No, Mom. It's to feed the sharks when I meet them."

Orly's mother stepped farther into the room and looked into her daughter's suitcase. Along with the chum, she saw five cans of tuna (they were closed), a pair of flippers, a snorkel and an inflatable shark fin.

"Where are your pajamas? Your shorts? Your underwear?"

Orly shrugged. "Mom, I packed the most *important* things first."

"A bag of fish guts?"

Orly stood up. She pointed to the big poster of a great white shark on the wall by her bed. "Shark researchers always travel with chum so they'll be able to signal sharks over to their boats. I've been following this team, Ocean Science, on their website. We can't lure

sharks with cereal or cookies. Come on, Mom."

Orly's mother shook her head. "We've talked about this, Orly. It's summer break. We always drive out to Grandma and Nana's cottage."

"I know. It's on the ocean. Where we can search for sharks!"

"You won't have so much time for sharks this year," Orly's mom said.

Orly narrowed her eyes. "What are you talking about?"

"I didn't want to give away the surprise so soon, but why not? We've signed you up for sailing camp! Isn't that exciting? You will finally be able to learn how to sail a boat."

Orly clapped her hands together. "Oh, I get it! First I learn how to steer a ship, and then I can help protect sharks on the open water!"

Orly's mom shook her head. "Uh, I don't think that's how this is going to work."

But Orly was already reaching into the backpack on her bed. She pulled out a tablet and turned it on. The screen lit up with a map of the ocean near the coast. There were lots of red dots marked on the screen. "The shark researchers from Ocean Science have been tracking this great white shark for months. Her name is Delta. She's close to where Grandma and Nana live. Isn't that so cool? I bet I'll actually be able to see her once I'm on the sailing ship!"

Orly's mother took the tablet and stared at the screen. "Those red dots are sharks?"

"I wish!" Orly said. "It's only one shark, Mom. Delta is wearing a tracker the scientists put on her. Every time she comes to the surface, Delta sends out a little ping that makes the red dot you see. Just look how close she is to the cottage! I'm sure I'll be able to meet Delta at some point."

Orly's mom stared at the dots. "That *is* pretty close," she said.

"She's looking for all the tasty seals in the water," Orly said. "You know, the ones that live on the rocks around the bend from Grandma and Nana's?"

Orly's mom stared at the shark poster by Orly's bed. The shark had its mouth open, and she could see all the sharp teeth in its mouth. She slowly handed the tablet back to her daughter. "Orly, I love that you're so excited about sharks.

But you need to remember three things. First, sailing camp is in the bay, away from the open water."

Orly nodded. "For now."

"Second, you are learning to sail teeny-tiny little sailboats. There are no ships, Orly. The biggest boat you will be on will be sailed by Dave, your sailing instructor."

"And lastly," Orly's mother said, pointing at the suitcase full of fish heads, "you aren't going anywhere without clothes! So give me the chum. I'll pack it and the tuna in my luggage. And don't forget your underwear!"

"The ones with the sharks on them?" Orly asked. She pulled a small pair of shark underwear out of her suitcase. "That was the *second* most important thing I packed!"

Chapter Two

It was a long, long, long drive to Grandma and Nana's cottage.

Orly had to share the back seat with her baby brother, Sebastian. That meant her parents kept putting on kiddie videos about teddy bears and fluffy kittens. It drove Orly crazy. "Mom, why can't I have my turn for something in the car?"

In the front seat Orly's dad shook his head. "Orly, you know that Sebastian needs something to calm him in the car.

You just want to watch nature videos about sharks."

"I know," Orly said. "Shark videos are THE BEST!"

"Those get him upset, and he isn't crying right now. He's not screaming. Can't we just enjoy the peace and quiet in the car for a minute?"

Orly turned and looked out the window. Fields and fields flew by, with no ocean in sight.

"This is soooooo boring," Orly said.

"Why don't you try counting interesting things that you see outside?" her father said.

Orly sighed and stared out her window. "Tree," she said. "Tree. Tree. Tree."

"That's a lot of trees," her father said.

Five hundred and eighty-two trees later, Orly fell asleep. When she woke up, her father was still driving. And there were still trees. No ocean in sight.

After twenty-three bathroom breaks and a long and sleepless night in a hotel, Orly and her family drove over a hill, and there it was. "The ocean!" Orly shouted.

Orly had been coming to the cottage with her family for as long as she could remember. She had learned to walk on the soft, sandy beach. She loved the feel of the cool waves crashing against her bare feet. She loved the smell of the salty wind and the way it whipped at her clothes. Sometimes, when it was foggy, she couldn't see anything. But today the sun was shining. The ocean was blue and endless, stretching on forever.

The car had barely come to a complete stop when Orly flung open the door and hopped out. She pulled off her shirt and threw it into the bushes. Underneath she was wearing her rainbow-striped bathing suit.

"Orly!" her mom said. "What are you doing?"

"I slept in my bathing suit and haven't taken it off."

"But you've been wearing it for over a whole day," her mother said.

Orly pulled off her pants and kicked them into another bush. "A shark researcher always wears her bathing suit," she said. "You never know when you're going to have to jump into the water."

Then Orly reached back into the car and pulled out her tablet. She flipped it open and turned it on. "I've been tracking Delta for the past four hours."

Orly's dad looked cross. "On our data plan?"

"You said it was for important stuff," Orly said. "Delta has pinged two times since breakfast. She's really close by. I'm going to see if we can spot her dorsal fin from the beach. See you!"

With that Orly began to race away from the cottage.

"Orly!" her father shouted. "Get back here. You haven't even said hello to your grandparents."

Orly stopped and turned. Standing at the front door of the cottage were Grandma and Nana. At the top of her lungs, she shouted, "Hellllooooo!"

And without giving them a hug, she tore off down the path leading to the beach.

Chapter Three

The next morning Orly woke up excited to go looking for Delta. She threw on her bathing suit, launched herself down the stairs and grabbed her tablet. She was wearing a gigantic pair of scuba goggles and carrying a pair of well-worn flippers.

"I'm off to the beach!" Orly announced to her family. They were all at the breakfast table, drinking coffee.

"Orly, the beach will have to wait until after camp today," her mom said. "We're going to take you to sailing camp this morning."

Orly scrunched her face into a big frown. She did not want to go to camp. Delta had pinged many times during the night, and Orly wanted to see how close to shore Delta would swim that day.

"I don't want to go to sailing camp. Delta needs me!" Orly explained.

"Sailing will put you on the water. Isn't that what you wanted?"

"But you said we won't be out on the ocean. And sailing camp won't teach me about shark tracking."

"Orly, you're not ready for the open ocean yet," said her mom. "Sailing camp will help you get used to being in a boat, and then later you can head out farther."

Orly shrugged. Maybe her mom was right.

"Besides, you haven't even tried sailing camp yet. You might really love it. We're all so excited for you to learn how to sail! I remember when I learned how to sail— it was so magical being on the water!"

Orly just wanted to find a way to get closer to Delta. If she could master being on a sailboat, then she might be ready for a larger boat. A shark scientist's boat. It was worth a try.

"Okay, I'll do it," Orly said.

"Great!" her mom said. "We leave right after breakfast."

"Hang on," Orly said. "I haven't even packed my shark explorer bag! Let me go upstairs and get it ready."

"I already packed your camp bag with everything you need."

"So you put in those bags of chum, right?"

Orly's mom shook her head. "No fish guts today, I'm afraid."

Orly thought about this. "You're right. I bet you can buy chum at the boathouse by the camp. We can save our chum to lure the sharks when I get home this afternoon!"

~~~

"Welcome to Camp Silver Sails."

Orly stood with a group of six kids near a pier where a bunch of small sailboats bobbed on the water. It was so foggy that Orly could not see the sea in the distance, just some rocks covered with seaweed close to the shore near the pier. Blocking her way onto the pier was a big man with red hair and thick arms. He flexed his muscles. He did not seem to mind how early it was. "I'm Dave, and I am your sailing instructor. Are you ready to hoist a silver sail?"

"But the sails aren't silver," Orly said, pointing to the boats.

The man turned around and stared at the boats. "It's just a name," he said.

Another boy raised his hand. "Why isn't it called Camp Golden Sails? Gold is worth *more* than silver!"

Orly nodded. "Or why not Camp Emerald Sails?!"

Dave squinted. "It's just Camp Silver Sails." He flexed his muscles again. "And who's ready to learn how to sail the seven seas?"

Most of the kids raised their hands. A little boy wearing a large sun hat, blue zinc cream on his nose and the biggest pair of sunglasses Orly had ever seen raised his hand. In a quiet voice he said "Um, excuse me? My mom promised me we would only be sailing in the bay. I get seasick with big waves and—"

Dave shook his head. "Ben, do not worry. I have already spoken to your mother. We are absolutely staying in the bay. The sea is too rough for all of you. We'll learn to sail where the water is calm. It's easier. *Safer*."

"But there are no sharks there," Orly said.

Dave nodded. "You're right. There are no sharks in the bay."

"Phew!" Ben said as he let out a big sigh. He was clearly relieved at this news.

Orly was not. "But we might get lucky," she said. All the other kids turned to look at her. "We might spot Delta nearby. You never know!"

"Who's Delta?" Ben asked.

"You haven't heard of Delta?!" Orly gawked. "She's just the coolest great white shark in the area!"

"There's a shark nearby?" Ben asked. His face grew pale. He began to twiddle nervously with the ends of his hair.

"Yeah," Orly said. "A great white!"

Dave walked over to Orly. Was he squinting again or just getting angry? "There are no sharks nearby."

"Phew!" Ben said. He did not like sharks.

The other kids looked at Dave. Then they looked at Orly.

"I know there's a shark nearby," Orly said.

"No there isn't," Dave said.

"Yes there is!" Orly said. She reached into her backpack and pulled out her tablet. She opened it to the app that showed where Delta the shark was. "See? Delta just pinged off the coast a few miles away."

The other kids leaned in closer and looked at Orly's tablet. Dave reached over and took the tablet out of Orly's hands.

"Hey, that's mine!" she exclaimed.

"You came here to learn how to sail—and to get away from screens," Dave told Orly. He put Orly's tablet into his backpack. "Don't worry. I'll keep it safe until the end of the day." Then he pointed to the boats tied to the pier. "Let me tell you all about a sailboat. That big pole is the mast, the front is called the bow, the back is called the stern. You steer your boat with a big rudder on the back…"

Orly watched the other kids follow Dave onto the pier.

All but one.

A boy who had been standing near Orly was still looking off at the water beyond the boats, just like Orly had been.

"Do you really think a shark will come right here?" he asked.

Orly shrugged. "No, not in this area. The water is too shallow, and all of the tasty seals are over by the rocks on the coast."

"That's too bad," the boy said. "Sharks are pretty cool."

Now it was the boy's turn to reach into his backpack and pull out something. It was a big book about ocean animals.

"Wow!" Orly said. "Where did you get that?"

"I brought it from home. These are all the endangered animals that live around here. I'm going to learn how to protect them. I know you like sharks, but there are also whales, dolphins, fish and plants that need our help." The boy closed the book and looked at Orly. "I'm Dean," he said with a big smile as he extended his hand.

Orly shook his hand. "Why do all those other creatures need our help? Are the sharks eating them?"

Dean shook his head. "No, it's worse than that. For starters, the ocean is getting more and more polluted. All the plastics we throw away and all kinds of chemicals end up in the water. I've been reading and watching specials about it."

Orly nodded. "My teacher did a few lessons about water pollution."

"But the whales are really in danger here," Dean said. "Did you know that this summer whales have been washing up onshore?"

"That's awful!"

"Sometimes they get stuck in fishing nets. I know that nobody is trying to hurt whales. That's why the fishermen have special trackers to let them know if whales are getting close. I have one of their apps on my phone."

"Right," Orly said, looking off toward Dave...and the tablet she'd brought from home.

"Hey, don't worry about Dave holding on to your tablet all day."

"I'm not worried. It's just that I want to know where Delta is going to be."

"Maybe I can help," Dean said. He reached again into his backpack and pulled out a small phone. "Look what I borrowed from home! It's my mom's old phone."

"She lets you use it?" Orly said.

"Yup," Dean said.

"And bring it onto a boat?"

"I think so," Dean said. "Why don't you show me how to load that shark-tracking app?"

"Sure thing," Orly said. Then she stopped and thought. "Unless you want to learn about how to tie knots with Dave."

Dean shrugged. "I can learn how to tie knots later. If Delta's nearby, we should totally track her now."

Chapter Four

After hearing Dave's stories about sailing across the ocean and several lessons on basic knot-tying, the kids were taken to the big sailboat. The fog had cleared, and the sun was shining.

"Whoa!" Orly said. Her jaw dropped as she looked at the big boat. "That boat is huge! I bet you could put a shark cage on the back of it if you wanted."

Ben moved away from Orly. "Sharks? I'd better make sure I'm prepared."

He pushed past Orly to the spot where the life jackets were. He took some extra ones and clipped them on his legs and arms. He looked like a giant orange marshmallow. He was about to put one on his head when Dave walked up to him.

"What are you doing?"

"Orly keeps talking about sharks," Ben said. "I don't want to get bitten by sharks. I don't want to fall into the water. I want to go home!"

Dave rolled his eyes. "We're not going anywhere near sharks," he said. "There are no sharks around here. Orly, stop making up stories."

"I'm not," Orly said. "You have my tablet. Why don't you check out the shark tracker? I bet Delta is close by. I've been staring at the water for a while now. I'm pretty sure I saw a dorsal fin in the distance."

"D-d-d-dorsal fin?" Ben said.

"There are no dorsal fins from sharks," Dave said.

"Then what did Orly see?"

"Maybe some dolphins. Or some seals playing in the water, kicking their flippers. There are tons of them in the area."

"Exactly!" Orly said. "Shark bait!"

Ben gulped.

"Don't worry," Dean said to Ben. "This boat is huge. It's totally safe."

"Exactly," Dave said. "You only need one life jacket. We're going to let our older students take us around the bay on a trip together. I expect everyone to show me how to tie those knots I showed you this morning."

"What knots?" asked Orly, clearly confused by having missed the morning lesson while she was talking to Dean and installing the tracking app on his phone.

Dave let out a big sigh as he turned away to help kids put on their life jackets.

The boat pitched back and forth on the water, and Orly's stomach felt like it was pitching back and forth too. It did not help that her bright-red life jacket was squishing her stomach tightly.

Ben had taken off most of his life jackets. He was looking over the edge of the boat as Orly came up to him.

"What are you looking at, Ben?" Orly asked. "Do you see any fish?"

As Ben turned around, Orly saw that his face had a bit of a green color. Ben let out a groan. "Yes, I see fish. The tuna sandwich I ate for lunch twenty minutes ago. Ugh. My stomach can't take this. This water is too wavy."

"Don't worry about Ben," Dave said. "He'll be okay. Most people get sick at the start of a boat trip. But you? *You* need to show me how to tie that knot."

"What knot?" Orly said.

"The one I showed you how to tie this morning," Dave said.

Orly bit her lip and tried to remember. But she'd been way at the back, showing Dean how to load up the shark-tracking app on his mom's phone. "Errr…" she said.

"You *were* listening to the lesson, right?"

"Oh sure," Orly said. She often tied her shoelaces in knots, so she tried to make the biggest, craziest knot she could.

"There you go!" she said and handed the rope to Dave.

Dave looked at Orly's knot and shook his head. "I guess that works," he said. "But how do you untie it?"

"You want me to *untie* it? Isn't it supposed to keep the sail tied up?"

From behind Orly there came a loud ping.

Dave narrowed his eyes. "What was that?"

Ping!

Orly's eyes went wide. "It's her! It's Delta! The Ocean Science app is working!"

"The shark?" Ben said. He leaned over the side of the boat and barfed again.

"Dean!" Orly cried. "Check your phone. Is the ping coming from it?"

Ping!

"Wow, that's a whole lot of pings!" Orly said. "That must mean Delta is close!"

Dean pulled out his phone and looked at the screen. He shook his head. "It's not coming from me."

Ping! Ping! Ping!

"It must be coming from my tablet. But Dave's got it," Orly said. She saw Dave's pack at the side of the boat, near where Ben was crouched. If she could only get to Dave's pack and get her tablet, then she could find Delta!

"Watch the sail," Orly told Dean. She pushed away from the mast and raced down the deck.

Ping! Ping!

Orly was almost at Dave's bag when Ben got up and reached into his pocket. He was right in Orly's path. She tried to leap past him, but she lost her balance and tripped over a big coil of rope on the deck.

Orly flew through the air, and—

SPLASH!

"ORLY!" Dave cried.

"Ewwww!" some of the kids on deck cried. "You fell right into Ben's barf water!"

Dave's eyes went wide. As quick as lightning, he snatched a life preserver off the side of the boat and jumped onto the edge. He was about to take a leap overboard to save Orly, but Orly held out a hand to stop him. "Don't worry, I'm fine," she said.

Dave stopped himself before jumping. "What?!"

"The water's great. Even with the barf. In fact, that will help attract the sharks! But what about all those pings? Is Delta around?"

Ben shook his head as he pulled out his phone. "Oh, that's just my phone. I was texting my mom to tell her I'm feeling sick. The pings were her telling me she's coming to pick me up. And that she's bringing me a change of clothes."

Dave shook his head and let out a deep sigh. He stepped back onto the deck and threw the life preserver into the water to pull Orly back aboard.

Dave shook his head. "This is sailing school, not *SCUBA* school, Orly. The point is to stay on the boat, not in the water. But let's turn back so Ben can go home."

"Do we have to?" Orly asked. "I just know we're going to come face-to-face with Delta!"

And at that, Ben let out a groan, doubled over at the side of the boat and barfed. Again.

Chapter Five

Dave went to speak with Orly's parents after they pulled up in their car. They'd left Sebastian back at the cottage with Grandma and Nana.

"You *jumped* off the boat?" Orly's dad asked.

Orly could see that her mom and dad were not pleased. They were standing with their arms folded across their chests. Orly's dad's eyebrows were pressed together in a frown.

"It was less of a jump and more of a fall," Orly said.

"You were looking for sharks," Orly's mom said. "You were not paying attention to Dave."

"People fall off boats all the time," Orly said. "That's why we wear life jackets and bathing suits."

"No," her dad said. "You were being irresponsible."

Orly threw up her hands in disbelief. "I went to camp just like you wanted!"

Orly was still upset when she and her parents got back to the cottage.

"Those lessons were expensive," Orly's mom said. "I loved sailing camp when I was your age. I learned the skills I needed so I could go on sailing trips with my moms. And if you practice, you'll be able to go on sailing trips with all of us too—and you'll be able to steer the boat as well."

Orly looked past her parents to Grandma and Nana. They were on the couch, rocking Sebastian to sleep.

"You've only had one day of camp, Orly," her mom said. "You can't give up this early."

"I'm not giving up," Orly said. "Boat skills will be important for when I'm a shark researcher. I will need my sea legs, but I also need to keep an eye on Delta."

Orly pulled out her tablet and turned on the shark tracker. "See?"

she said. "She is so close. But look at this other app I loaded up—there are a bunch of fishing boats right where she is feeding." Orly showed her mom and dad the dots on the two electronic maps. One showed where the shark was. The other showed where fishing boats were anchored.

"The scientists who study Delta are worried that she might get caught by the fishermen."

"I know you're worried about Delta, but she will be okay," her dad said. "She's not what the fishermen are trying to catch. And she goes after seals, not fish, so she should be safe."

Orly shook her head.

"Orly, here's the deal. If you make it all the way through Camp Silver Sails, we will sign you up for scuba camp when you're done."

Orly's eyes lit up. "Really?"

"But you have to stay on the boat," her mom said. "And you have to listen to Dave. All week long."

"But all we did was tie knots."

"All. Week. Long."

"Okay," Orly said. "I can do that."

"Who was that boy you were sitting with on the boat?"

"Oh, that's Dean," Orly said.

"What were you talking about?"

"You know, sharks—"

"Of course," Orly's dad said.

"But not just sharks."

"No?"

"Dean loves all ocean animals."

Her dad smiled. "Even the ones that sharks eat?"

Orly nodded. "He's worried about them. He keeps telling me about how we're polluting the water, and how they're in danger. He wants to save the animals."

"And not just the sharks?"

"No," Orly said. "He wants to save sharks and other animals, like whales and dolphins and seals. They're also in danger from all the people working in their habitat. Here, give me your tablet. Dean told me about all the apps we can download to track them too."

Orly's dad pulled his tablet away. "No, Orly. You have so many programs on here that I can't even find my Netflix button."

"But this is important," Orly said. "It's a matter of life and death! It's not just sharks that are in trouble. It's dolphins. And whales!"

Orly's dad opened his mouth to speak. He raised his finger like he always did when he was making a point. But then he stopped. "I've got an idea," he said. He pointed at the tablet. "But you'll have to show me where to find the Netflix button."

"Oh, that's easy," Orly said, taking the tablet from her dad and scrolling through it. She hit a button, and the menu screen opened up. "You want to watch all the scary movies, right?"

Orly's dad shook his head. He scrolled through some of the programs.

Orly could see pictures of nature shows about animals and the earth. Her dad clicked on a button. "Let's learn about this together," he said with a smile.

Chapter Six

After watching a nature show about coral reefs with her dad, Orly had big questions. She called Dean and told him what she had learned. They agreed that Dave might have some answers. He knew all about boats. He might know about the ocean too!

The next morning Dave looked tired. He had dark circles under his eyes.

"What are we doing to help rescue all the endangered animals?" Orly asked.

"This is sailing school," Dave said. "We are learning to use the rudder to steer the boat."

Orly shook her head.

Dean piped up. "What we *should* be learning is how to untie all the fishing nets that the turtles and dolphins are getting caught in."

"That should be our next lesson," Orly said.

Dave shook his head. "You're right about wanting to help those animals, but we're not going to sail out to stop fishermen from doing their jobs."

"Then we should stop eating seafood!" Orly said.

Ben asked, "You don't want us to eat fish again? Ever?"

"I don't think that's what she's saying." Dave sighed.

Ben kept focused on Orly. "I'm going out for lobster dinner tonight. What am I supposed to eat? A baked potato?"

"As long as it doesn't come wrapped in foil or plastic," Dean said.

"What do you mean?"

"Look at our lunches," Orly said. She pointed at Ben's backpack. "Go on. Open it up!"

Dave shook his head. "It's 9:00. It's not even snack time yet. Don't you want to learn how to use the rudder?"

Ben looked from Dave and then to Orly.

"I bet you that lunch is full of plastic packaging," said Dean.

Ben looked at his backpack. He unzipped it and pulled out his lunch bag. He removed all the things inside the bag. There was an apple. A juice box with a straw, a granola bar, a package of cookies and a snack pack of cheese and crackers with plastic wrap covering it.

Orly scowled. "How can you even think about eating that lunch?"

"Because we're hungry?" one of the kids said.

Ben shrugged. "That's what I eat every day," he said.

"I watched a bunch of specials about our garbage. Do you know where that plastic goes?" Orly said.

"In the garbage," Ben said.

"Exactly!" Dean added. "And where does the garbage go?"

"In the dump," Ben said.

"Some of it does. But do you know how much of our garbage goes into the ocean?"

Ben shook his head.

"Eighteen billion pounds a year!"

"You're kidding me," Ben said.

"And that plastic does not break down," Dean said. "It just floats around. Animals and fish sometimes eat it."

"Ugh," Ben said. He leaned over the side of the boat and groaned.

"That's better," Orly said. "Fish can totally eat barf." She smiled. "Plus, maybe you can lure Delta to our boat!"

Dave stepped over to Orly and Dean. "Enough, guys. You are right about the plastic, but you're upsetting Ben and the other students."

"They *should* be upset!" Dean said. "This is a matter of life or death for ocean animals."

"It's more a matter of you and Orly helping out at the back of our boat," Dave said.

"The back of the boat?"

"Sure," Dave said with a smile. "You can look out for whales or dolphins."

Orly scowled at Dave's comment, but then she turned to the back of the boat. A bunch of the students' backpacks were there. Her eyes lit up. She went over to Dean and whispered something in his ear.

Dean nodded. "This sounds like a good idea," he said.

They stayed at the stern of the boat while Dave took the boat around the bay. He showed the other kids how to use the mast and the sail and pointed out some of the animals.

Some time later the rest of the students were at the front of the ship, looking at the cormorants nesting on rocks at the edge of the bay. Dean and

Orly sat together at the stern, beside a heap of sandwiches, cookies, granola bars, crackers, cakes and juice boxes. Beside the food pile was a large plastic bag filled with all the packaging that had been removed from the various lunches.

At the front of the boat Dave raised his voice and announced, "Okay, sailors, time for lunch! Please head to the stern and collect your lunch bags!"

The students started to move toward the back of the boat, where Orly and Dean were seated with proud expressions on their faces.

Ben stopped in his tracks. "Hey, where's my lunch? My mom made sure to pack me lots of crackers to help my tummy settle. Where are they?"

Ben looked at the pile of food beside Orly and Dean. His eyes went from his

lunch bag to the food, and then to the collected packaging.

Orly got up and strode toward the others. "Excuse me!" she said. "Dean and I have been busy trying to support ocean wildlife this morning. In order to make sure that no plastics went into the open water, we took off all the packaging, so that everyone can eat without worrying about it going overboard! You're welcome!"

Dave looked at the pile of food. His eyes darted from Orly to Dean. He took a deep breath. "You two are in a whole lot of trouble," he said. "How will anyone know which is their lunch? What about kids with allergies who need their food separated? This is a disaster!"

Just then Ben turned and pointed at something behind the group.

"What is it now, Ben?" Dave asked.

"The sail! Look, it's really going!"

Before Dave could say anything else, the huge gust of wind that had opened the sail blew across the deck of the boat. The kids stumbled to keep their balance.

"Oh no," Orly said. She turned to the big bag of plastic waste.

But it was too late.

The wind blew the bag right over the edge of the boat. The bag splashed down into the bay, and the plastic packaging started spreading out on the surface of the water.

"The animals!" Dean cried.

"Don't worry," Orly said, watching the plastic drifting away. "I've got this!"

Making sure her life jacket was strapped on, Orly stood on the edge of the deck, then turned around to give Dean a thumbs-up.

"Not again," Dave said.

SPLASH!

Orly swam through the water. She reached out to grab the bits of plastic with her hands. She turned back to everyone on the boat. "Come on in and help!" she shouted. "It's only a matter of time before the turtles come and try eating this."

Everybody stood where they were on the deck.

Everybody, that is, except Dave. He kicked off his shoes, put on his life jacket and jumped into the water.

"Great!" Orly exclaimed. "Dave, I'm glad you're thinking about the animals first."

Dave paddled over to Orly and grabbed her by the back of her life jacket. He pulled her back toward the boat.

"Hey! What are you doing?"
"I'm thinking about your safety—and my job!" he said angrily.

Once she was back on board, Orly was made to sit at the side of the boat. Dave paced back and forth. "Orly, you and Dean are dry-docked for tomorrow."

"Dry-docked? What's that?"

"It means you are sitting on the dock to think about your actions," Dave said.

"What, you mean helping out sea animals?" Orly asked.

"Tearing apart lunches. Jumping off boats. Not following safety rules! You will stay on the dock tomorrow as a consequence."

"Okay," Orly said. "That sounds fine."

"*And* I'm going to have to call your parents."

Orly gulped. They weren't going to like this!

Chapter Seven

Orly's parents definitely did not like what Dave had to say.

"You jumped off the boat *again*?" Orly's dad asked later that afternoon.

"I know how that sounds," Orly said.

"It sounds like you're not trying your best," Orly's dad said.

"But I am!" Orly shouted. "You and I watched that show about the oceans. We saw how much plastic was getting into the water. I was just trying to help!"

"And now you can help from the dock."

The next day, while Dave had the rest of the kids on the boat, Orly and Dean had to sit at the end of the pier. Dave gave them some handouts about boat safety to study. He also gave them two big piles of rope and instructed them to practice tying knots.

Orly kicked at her rope. This was not how she wanted to spend her day at all.

"At least it's sunny," Dean said.

Then a bank of fog rolled in.

"Maybe we'll get lucky and not get rained on," Dean said.

Then it started to rain.

"Maybe you should stop talking for a second," Orly said. She looked down at the paper Dave had given them to study. "How are we supposed to help animals with all of this paper?"

"By reading it?" Dean said.

"I know how to put on a life jacket," Orly said. "This is silly. I'm going on strike!"

"How can you go on strike at a sailing camp?"

Orly looked down at the markers and papers and smiled.

~~~

A while later Dave's sailboat cut through the fog, as he brought it back to the pier for the kids to have lunch.

Ben, who still looked sick and the same green as the seaweed coating the rocks, pointed ahead. "Look! It's Orly and Dean. They're holding something."

The other students strained to see what Orly and Dean were doing. All they could see were two people marching back and forth through the fog, holding papers in their hands.

"Please tell me they managed to stay dry on the dock this whole time," Dave said. As they grew closer to the shore, it was easier to make out what was on Orly's paper. "I hope it's not about sharks again."

"Sharks?" Ben cried, looking around at the water. "Did someone say sharks?"

"Sails hurt whales!" Orly and Dean chanted together. Dean had written the words on his piece of paper and kept chanting it loudly. "Sails hurt whales! Sails hurt whales!"

Orly held up the sheet of paper Dave had given her. On it was a picture of a boat, but Orly had crossed it out and put a big skull and crossbones on it.

"Sails *don't* hurt whales," Dave said as he tied the boat to the pier and helped the other kids off. "We rarely use the engine. And we are rarely out as far as where the large marine animals are."

"But Dave," Orly said, "did you know that whales are getting hurt from all the big ships in these waters?"

"Guys, I know how animals can get hurt from fishing and from boats. I'm learning about marine biology at the university in the city. This is my summer job. I *also* want to save animals. That's why I learned how to sail and how to be safe around boats."

"Oh," Orly said.

"I did not know that," Dean said. He folded up his sign. He put it in his pocket.

Dave took a deep breath. He looked at the kids around him. "Tell you what," he said. "Why don't we all have lunch, and then I'll take you to one of my special research sites? It's an island away from the bay, near a peninsula with lots of seabirds and seals."

"No way!" Dean said.

"Seals," Orly said with a smile. "Do you know what *eats* seals?"

"Please don't say it," Ben said as he put a finger to his lips. "Shhhhhh..."

"—ARKS!" Orly finished.

Chapter Eight

The open ocean was wavy and bumpy, and maybe not the best place to be right after eating lunch. Already Ben was feeling sick again. Even Orly's stomach felt like it had twenty butterflies fluttering around in it. But she kept her eyes on water in the distance, like Dave had told her to. That made her feel less dizzy. It also meant that Orly kept getting sprayed in the face with salty seawater.

Then Orly spotted something up ahead. It was a rocky island, the one Dave had told them about.

"There it is," Dave said. He let the wind out of the sail and stood at the bridge of the boat. He steered the boat around the edge of the rocky island. Waves crashed against the dark, jagged rocks. Flocks of birds flew in the salty air. Several seals were making noise as they basked on some of the large flat rocks on the island. They did not seem upset by Dave and the kids sailing by.

Dean stood up and stared at the rugged island. "Wow," he said. "It's like something from a pirate movie." He turned to Dave. "Can we go looking for treasure there?"

Dave shook his head. "No, we can't go onto the island. First, it is a protected site where animals are safe from people. But second, the waves are too rough, and the island is too rocky. We would crash the boat before we set foot on the island."

"Crash?" Ben said with a whimper. He pulled out his phone. "Do I need to call my mom again?"

"Don't worry, we're not going to crash," Dave said. "But look! Do you see those birds at the far end of the island? Those are puffins," he said.

Everybody looked where Dave was pointing.

"Not too many puffins come around these parts. But a few of them nest on this island in the summer."

"Cool," one of the kids said. "And what's that?" They were pointing past the island. It looked like the clouds were moving in toward them.

"A fog bank," Dave said. "Coming in fast too."

In a few moments the boat was swallowed up by the thick white fog.

"Great," another student said. "No puffins."

Ben shook his head. "Are we going to get lost in this?"

"Nah," Dave said. "A good sailor knows how to use a compass." He went back to the steering wheel and gave it a turn.

Ping!

Orly's eyes went wide.

Ping! Ping!

Orly looked at Ben, who was trying to keep from losing the rest of his lunch. She walked to where he was hanging over the side of the boat. "Is that your phone?" she asked Ben.

Ben shook his head and held up his phone. "Nope. I was going to use it to take pictures of the birds, but I can't do much with all this fog."

Ping!

Orly went over to Dean. Dean pulled his cell phone from his pocket and stared at it. "It's Delta!"

"Where?" Orly stared out to sea, trying to spot the shark's big fin. But all she could see was the fog around them. "Great! Our first real shark sighting, and we can't see a thing!"

Ben pushed toward the middle of the boat. "D-d-do you think it could jump on board?"

Orly's eyes went wide. "You know, I saw a show where something like that happened. We could get a real close look at Delta then!"

Ben whimpered and moved closer to Dave, who was busy trying to turn the boat around.

Orly squinted, trying to see anything close by. The phone was pinging really loudly. The shark must be close! Then Orly saw something dark pop out of the water just by the boat. It was too foggy for her to get a good look at it. Was it a shark? Was it Delta?

Then the shape was gone!

The phone pinged again.

There it was again—even *closer* to the boat now. It was something dark and furry.

Since when did sharks get furry? The creature went under the water. When it came up again, Orly got a better look at its face full of whiskers and its black eyes. And then Orly knew what it was. "Look!" Orly said. "It's a *seal!*"

Ping!

The seal went underwater and then came back up again.

Ping! Ping!

"Why is that seal pinging?" Dean said. "Did Ocean Science put a shark tracker on the seal?"

Orly looked at the seal. It was missing one of its back flippers!

The seal gave a cry. It went under again.

It did not come back up.

"Do you think…" Dean started. "Is Delta hunting the seal?"

Ping!

"Shark!" Orly said.

"Shark?" Ben cried.

Dave turned the wheel and angled the boat away from the fog. "No, no," he said. "No sharks."

"It is! It's Delta!" Orly cried. "He's pinging all over the place."

Ping!

Dean looked down at his phone. "It's Delta, all right. The tracker says that Delta is, like, RIGHT HERE WITH US!"

The fog was getting thinner. Dave steered the boat out of it.

Now Orly looked over the side of the boat. They were surrounded by dark water and by splashes of white where the waves hit the rocks. It was too difficult to see down below for any sign of Delta. "But I don't see him."

Ping!

"It's just that seal," Dean said.

The seal came up on the other side of the boat. Orly saw it bobbing up and down in the waves. Then she saw something wedged in the back of the remaining flipper. It was a small plastic tag with a metal tube sticking out of it. "The tracker!" Orly said. "It's Delta's tracker!"

Ping! Ping!

"Look, Dave! That seal has Delta's tracker in her other flipper."

Dave cupped his hands over his eyes and stared at the seal. "I think you're right," he told Orly. He looked at her and gave a nod. "She must have hooked onto it when she was in a scrape with Delta. That was really well spotted."

"What do we do?" Ben said.

Dave turned to Orly. "You found it. What do you think, Orly? What would a good marine biologist do?"

"Why are you asking *me*?"

"Because," Dave said with a bit of a smile, "*you're* the one who found the seal. Nicely done, Orly!"

Orly stood there, staring at the seal as it bobbed up and down in the water. "We can't just leave it here like this," she said.

Dave shook his head.

"I know!" Orly said. She grabbed the phone from Dean's hands and activated the app for Delta's researchers. "We can call the scientists who are following Delta. It says their boat is not far from here."

"Are we saving the seal?" Ben asked.

"Yes," Orly said with a big grin.

"Too bad you can't save my lunch," Ben said.

Chapter Nine

Not too long after that another boat came into view. But this was no sailboat! It was a large boat with the words *OCEAN SCIENCE* stamped on its side. Orly could not believe her eyes. All kinds of people were on board. And there were even two shark cages!

"Oh no," Ben said, staring at the shark cages.

"Oh *yes!*" Orly and Dean said together.

One of the scientists climbed down the side of the boat and sat down in an inflatable dinghy. She steered the dinghy over to where the sailboat and the seal were.

"Hi, Dave," the woman called out. She did not seem to mind being on the open ocean, bobbing up and down in a tiny boat.

She threw a rope over to Dave, who pulled the dinghy close to the sailboat so she could climb on board. She was soaking wet and had on a big life jacket. "I heard somebody found Delta's tracker on a seal," she said.

"It was Orly!" Dean said, pointing to her.

The woman smiled and shook Orly's hand. "My name is Jessica. I'm the marine biologist who tagged Delta. I'm glad you

found the tracker. It would cost a lot of money to replace. And this brave seal got away from Delta. We can make sure the seal heals up."

The kids stared at Jessica. They watched as she leaned over the edge of the sailboat and used a special tool to grab the tracker from the seal's hind flipper.

"Wow!" Orly said.

Jessica held up the tracker for the kids to see. Then she gave Dave a high five. "Dave and I work together at the university."

Orly could not believe what she was hearing. "You. *Work*. With. Dave?!"

Dave grinned. "I bet you never saw that one coming, did you, Orly?"

Orly shook her head.

"Tell you what," Jessica said. "Since Orly did such a great job of finding the tracker, maybe you guys would like to come and join us on our boat tomorrow. We're out hunting for Delta and other other great white sharks to tag and study."

Orly and Dean looked at each other. And then they screamed.

Jessica turned to Dave. "Are they okay?"

~~~

That night Orly's grandma and nana took the whole family out to a big, fancy restaurant in town. Orly's parents ordered delicious lobster dinners for everybody.

"But it's not my birthday until the end of the month," Orly said. "Why are we here tonight?"

"We are very proud of you, Orly," said her mom.

"You are?"

"You stuck with sailing school. And, as it turns out, that shark app on the tablet was helpful."

"And you saved the seal," her dad said.

"*And* Delta's tracker," Orly said.

"Exactly," said Orly's mom. "It turns out you are more responsible than we thought. And you will need to be responsible when we sign you up for scuba lessons."

Orly gulped.

"Scuba lessons?"

"Oh yes, they start next week," said her dad. "We even found you the perfect instructor." Then he smiled and pointed to a table just behind Orly. "Look, there he is right now."

Orly turned.

Her mouth dropped open. "No. Way."

There sat Dave. He waved at her from his table, where he was eating with Jessica and some of the other scientists from the Ocean Science boat.

Dave took the paper straw out of his drink and stuck it in his mouth. He turned it upside down so it looked like a snorkel. "I hope you are ready," Dave said. "Because starting Monday, I am going to teach you how to scuba dive!"

"YESSSSS!!!!" Orly screamed, jumping away from the table and leaping about the restaurant. Everybody turned and stared at her. "Sharks! We are going to go under the water and see sharks!"

"Whoa," Dave said. "Easy there. Before we go underwater, we need to teach you about how much weight to put on your belt to keep you from surfacing."

"Sure, sure…"

"And your wet suit."

"Uh-huh…"

"And teach you how to use the regulator."

"Right…"

"And check that your air tank is working properly."

Orly looked at Dave. "We do get to go under the water, right?"

Dave flashed Orly a big grin. "Eventually," he said.

Jeff Szpirglas and **Danielle Saint-Onge** are married, live together in Kitchener, Ontario, and teach in classrooms with students of diverse cultural backgrounds. Jeff has written several books and enjoys writing scary fiction like *Tales from Beyond the Brain* and *Tales from the Fringes of Fear*. Danielle has a master's degree in social anthropology and is a crusader for equity in the classroom. Besides teaching, they spend their time writing stories and taking care of their twins.